ISOLATION TALES

Melanie Stephens

CONTENTS

A little about the Contagion of 2020

This disease is part of a large family of viruses which may cause illness in animals or humans. In humans, several are known to cause respiratory infections ranging from the common cold to more severe diseases such as Middle East Respiratory Syndrome (MERS) and Severe Acute Respiratory Syndrome (SARS).

A new virus and disease were unknown before the outbreak began in Wuhan, China, in December 2019. Currently, we do not know the source but all available evidence suggests that it has a natural animal origin and is not a constructed virus. At this stage, it is not possible to determine precisely how humans in China were initially infected.

This new sickness is mainly transmitted through droplets

generated when an infected person coughs, sneezes, or speaks. These droplets are too heavy to hang in the air. They quickly fall on floors or surfaces. You can be infected by breathing in the virus if you are within 1 metre of a person who carries it, or by touching a contaminated surface and then touching your eyes, nose or mouth before washing your hands.

By April 2020, just over four months since the outbreak began, over 210,000 people lost their lives to this virus all over the world, and over 3.1 million people have been infected. Several sources suggest due to under reporting of the virus, these numbers could be as much as 60% higher than recorded.

Source: The World Health Organisation

Courage isn't having the strength to go on - it is going on when you don't have strength.

NAPOLEON BONAPARTE

Below is a list of the **Key Workers** that carried on going to work, putting themselves at risk for others.

- Doctors
- Nurses
- Midwives
- Paramedics
- Social workers
- Care workers
- Other frontline health and social care staff including volunteers

- Support and specialist staff
- Producers and distributors of medicine and equipment
- Nursery staff
- Teaching staff
- Social workers
- Certain specialist professionals
- Justice system
- Religion
- Charities
- Other key frontline services
- Death management
- Journalists and broadcasters providing public service broadcasting
- Police and support staff

- Ministry of Defence civilians, contractors and armed forces personnel
- Fire and rescue service employees and support staff
- National Crime Agency staff
- Border security
- Prison and probation staff
- Other national security roles including overseas
- Local government
- Public transport
- Some bank, building society and financial market workers
- Oil, gas, electricity, water and sewerage workers

- IT and data infrastructure workers
- Civil nuclear workers
- Chemicals workers
- Telecommunications workers, including network, engineering, call centres, IT etc
- 999 and 111 critical services
- Postal services and delivery
- Payment providers
- Waste disposal workers

You are the beating heart of our nation. Thank you.

A New Arrival

I am born, where can I go?

Ooh, you look nice, I'll say hello!

I'll visit for a while, see what you do,

Oh, who's that? I've grown in two!

And another person, this is fun,

I want to expand, explore every one.

I can exist in whoever comes by

I think I might travel, I'm ready to fly.

So many of me already, this is great!
Let's go!

I like that I can hide, spread wide
before you know.

I am all over the globe now, I've
multiplied so fast.

All I see is ageless prey, not how long
they will last.

I evolve into a killer, without much effort or thought

I love to observe what chaos I have brought.

They are trying to contain me, keep people alive,

But these people are stupid, watch me thrive!

I will conquer the world, you can't stop me, screw your bans

Hey! Wait a minute! Stop that! Stop washing your hands!

Don't listen to others! Don't stay inside!

Stay close to each other, no need to hide.

Millions will know me, I bring sickness and death,

I will be looking for more bodies as you take your last breath.

The Fireman

'Please don't go. Stay home Frank, just this once.'

'Rosie, you know I can't. There are too many guys off, we're down to a skeleton crew as it is.'

Rosie watched helplessly as Frank threw a couple of apples inside his backpack on the worktop. 'But there must...'

'No, I'm sorry darling but even Farley's down and he came to work when his appendix was bursting.' Frank turned around and looked at the floor as he spoke. 'It's putting the guys' lives at risk if I don't go.'

Rosie ran her hands over her perfectly formed round belly. 'I'm scared Frank. I'm scared that you won't come home.'

Frank sighed and placed his hands on her shoulders as he studied her eyes. Without a hint of make-up, Rosie's eyelashes were long and full. Her face was glowing. Frank wanted to kiss her, protect her. His jaw clenched, he knew he had to leave. 'That's just your hormones talking. Come on babe, you know I can't pick and choose. I got to go.'

Rosie shrugged his hands away and stepped back. 'You shouldn't even be out there! You have one lung and you're diabetic. You're high risk!'

'Everyone's at risk, Rosie. You're vulnerable.'

'Exactly! You could pass on the virus to me or the baby.' She knew it was a cheap shot, and Rosie regretted it as soon as the words left her mouth.

'DON'T YOU THINK I KNOW THAT!?!' Frank grabbed his backpack and flung it over his shoulder. 'Sorry love, but I can't let people die just because I'm afraid. I must go. I love you.'

His body felt tense and heavy as he stepped toward her. Rosie crossed her arms as he leaned in and wrapped them around her. She slowly moved hers across his back.

'It's so unfair.' She whispered into his ear.

Frank gradually pulled away. 'I know. I hate it too.'

He kissed his wife on the forehead and strode out the back door.

An hour later he was riding with his crew towards a block of flats just outside his district. Frank rubbed his eyes, broken sleep continued to torment him. The fire the truck was travelling to was big. Another fire department was trying to control the blaze, but it was way too big for them and Frank's Unit had been called upon to help. As he sat there his body sank to the seat, the weight of his uniform felt thick and solid. Before Frank could stop it, the thought of never meeting his son entered his head. He shook his head swiftly to make it vanish.

Captain Frank Bardot got out of the truck and started setting up the equipment they might need with his team. The District Chief Fire Officer, of Frank's unit, Jesse Helmsworth went to the other Chief to plan a strategy.

Jesse came back to Frank and the team to brief them on the size of the building and the equipment they would be using.

'Do we know what started it all?' asked Lieutenant Cliff Flynn.

'Turns out there are two care workers in these flats, they think two kids set fire to it because the daft sods think the workers are carriers of the virus infecting the neighbourhood.'

Cliff shook his head. 'Bloody hell. This virus lockdown is bringing out the worst in people, isn't it? Are the care workers out?'

'Not yet. They were working on their floors next. There are about thirty people still inside. Let's get to work.'

The Chief gave the crew details on where to go and so they entered the flats. Darkness thick with dense grey smoke surrounded them. Frank's senses magnified as the adrenaline took over his body. Sounds from all around him spoke at once, the walls creaked, and the timber cracked as the heat from the blaze engulfed every part of him.

The radio cackled as the Chief tried to guide them through the scorching inferno.

The team took out heat sensor cameras. Frank wiped his shield to see the thermal imaging clearer. These were their eyes, and the main tool they had to find people and save lives.

'Over here Frank!' Cliff called, pointing to a staircase in the corner.

'Floor 3. I repeat floor 3.' The chief instructed over the radio.

'Frank?' Cliff called behind him.

Frank held up three fingers to show he had heard the message and they ascended the stairs. There was no way to know how long the stairs would hold for, so they had to move fast.

On the third floor, he could hear a woman screaming and children crying. Frank, and Cliff, followed the sound to a flat and kicked in the door. It slammed to the ground. They took out the devices for heat senses and used the thermal cameras to locate where the screaming was coming from. Every second was precious. The mother was huddled over her children like a roman shield, trying to protect them as best she could. The children were barricaded beneath her strong protective arms, their faces buried close to her chest. She shook her son who seemed to be sleeping but would not wake up. Frank leaned in and felt for a pulse. It was there, but faint.

As Frank lifted the boy in his arms, the mother pulled on his sleeve.

'Please, my husband! He's isolating away from us. He has the virus.'

'Where is he?' Frank said.

'Back bedroom.'

Frank gave the boy to Cliff and told him to get the mother, child and boy out of there.

'The kid needs an ambulance. There's one more.'

'Okay, Stay safe. See you down there.' Cliff called as he carried the unconscious boy and led the children and mother out of the door.

Frank took out his radio. 'One in bedroom. Going in solo. Cliff on way.'

He went to find the back bedroom.

The door was closed. Frank kicked his way through it and found a man in the foetal position on the bed.

'Stay away, I have the virus!' he cried.

'It's okay mate. I got you.'

As Frank scooped the man up, he broke into a coughing fit and could not stop. Frank carried him out of the bedroom into the lounge and back out through the front door.

Frank saw fellow firefighters clutching people in front of him and moving swiftly to the staircase.

'Stay with me mate,' Frank said.

The man huddled close to his saviour. His mouth repeated five words in a loop. 'Save me God. Save me.'

Frank held him tighter. 'You'll be okay mate. I'm here.'

He descended the stairs as if his feet were light and full of air. When he came outside, clear air and surroundings welcomed Frank, but he found he felt the weight he was carrying. He found the ambulance crew, climbed inside and put the man on a stretcher.

'He has the virus,' he told them as his arms became free.

The ambulance crew nodded and thanked him as he walked away. He tried to find Cliff in the crowd and automatically started to walk toward the blaze.

The Chief came over to him.

'Are you okay Frank?' Jesse asked

'Sure, boss. Got them out. Just going to go back in for the others.'

'Let's get you a different helmet before you do. This one's cracked right through.'

A New Definition of Desperation

As the young man opened the doors to the crowd pressed up against the glass, Brenda lunged forward using her handbag as an extra weapon as she bashed strangers out of her way. A lady pushed Brenda sideways almost causing her to fall to the ground.

I'll teach her Brenda thought. She looped the strap from her bag and tripped the woman up. The woman swore as she plummeted to the floor and Brenda grinned as she got to her feet.

She raced through the aisles of the supermarket, toward the household cleaning section and found what she'd been looking for. A jumbo 24 pack of toilet rolls. She picked up two.

'One per customer,' a shelf stacker informed her wearily from across the aisle.

'I need two! You can't get...'

'I'm afraid we can't sell you more than one. It's customer policy.' He said in a monotone voice. 'You will have to come back tomorrow if you need two. Although, unless you have twenty-four kids, I don't imagine you will need more that soon.'

Brenda clasped the jumbo packs close to her chest. 'I waited an hour this morning!'

'I'm sorry, but as I say it's customer policy.'

'Sonofabitch!'

'It's not my fault madam.'

'Sorry, yes I know you are doing a super job.'

The shelf-stacker half smiled at her out of politeness. By the time Brenda looked again, the shelf was empty. She reluctantly put one of the jumbo packs back and immediately it was gone. Picked up by another desperate shopper.

Right, Brenda thought, *what else do I need? Flour? Baking aisle!*

Brenda ran as fast as she could, her jumbo pack of loo roll banged against her leg with every step. She found the shelf she wanted and then her heart sank. It was empty. She looked around, hoping, praying for something. Then Brenda spotted it. A premium luxury Italian blend flour. She looked at the price of £6.27. Fuck.

Then she felt a presence beside her. Another woman. Shit! They looked at each other for a moment and then both reached the shelf. They grabbed for it at the same time and the bag ripped covering them both in white powder and dust. Her opponent sneezed.

'SHE'S GOT THE VIRUS!' someone screamed.

Brenda scarpered to the next aisle leaving the woman covered in flour to explain herself. Brenda started running up and down aimlessly looking for anything to jump out at her that could be classed as a necessity. The only thing she found was a 75cl bottle of Vodka and a Chicken Korma ready meal for one. Neither she nor her husband could stand Indian food, but it was all she could get. Armed with her urgent supplies of vodka, the meal no one wanted and a jumbo pack of loo roll, Brenda made her way to the till. Waiting for the cashier to be free, Brenda also picked up three Kinder eggs, five Mars bars and two multipacks of Spearmint chewing gum, just in case they ran out of toothpaste.

The cashier greeted her and totalled up her shopping. £23.84. What a waste of money.

Brenda got home in a slump. She ate a Mars bar in the car to give herself a chocolate hit but it didn't work. Her husband Harry glanced up half-heartedly whilst playing a football game on the PlayStation.

'Hey love, I'm in the final! How was the supermarket?'

'Complete shit. Did you want a Mars bar or a Kinder egg?'

'Kinder egg? What did you buy those for? We're not six years old for fuck's sake! GOAL!'

Brenda rolled her eyes and chucked him a Mars bar. She pulled out her freezer drawer and moved several things around to make room for the Chicken Korma for one. She

put the loo roll multipack in the spare room with the rest of them.
Brenda made herself a cup of tea and ate a kinder egg. She enjoyed making the toy, she debated whether to show Harry but thought better of it.

Instead, she got out her phone and browsed the supermarket delivery slots. They might as well have had a clown laughing at her for even trying. Every time was fully booked for the next six weeks.

Brenda tried googling food supplies; the usual search results appeared. On a whim, she went to page 8. There was a company called Overstock Tastier Foods. Clicking on the link, she could not believe what she saw. They had large quantities of everything and could deliver the next day. Amazing!

She spent two hours scouring the website, devouring everything like Augustus Gloop with Willy Wonka's chocolate river. Everything was in stock and so cheap. This was brilliant! Half tempted to message her friends about the golden nugget she had found, Brenda selfishly decided to keep it to herself. Brenda placed the order and readily entered her credit card details.

The next day she sat by the window waiting eagerly for the van to appear. Two in the afternoon, it finally came, and the delivery guy came out and opened the back doors. The box he carried was smaller than she expected, but she just assumed they packed it well. The man left it on the doorstep for her. Brenda found she could lift it easily. She brought it into the kitchen and enthusiastically tore open the box.

Brenda opened the flaps and felt deflated. Everything she ordered was in there just a tiny version of it. Instead of a loaf of bread, there were three slices in a sealed pack, instead of washing up liquid, there was a tiny travel size bottle of it. In place of a pack of chocolate chip cookies, there was a pack of two like you receive in hotels. Furiously, Brenda grabbed her phone to find the email of the company to give

them a piece of her mind. Then she saw it.
It wasn't Overstock Tastier Foods it was *Overstock Taster Foods*. They were all taster products and testers left over by promotions by companies which is why they were so cheap.   Brenda sighed, and put the tiny groceries away before making herself a cup of tea and cheering herself up with another Kinder egg. There was no toy to make this time, just a little figure of a pig eating.

'What fucking irony.' Brenda said crossly and threw the pig into the lounge, hitting her husband Harry on the head.

An Extreme Routine Absence

Dear Mum,

It's so awful not to talk to you properly and instead send you this letter. You have always been my sounding wall and I really miss our teatime chats where I can just offload. I'm so glad you had a nice birthday, one to remember I suppose, as the only one you have ever spent in a lockdown. I know we couldn't do our annual afternoon tea, but I'm glad you like the book and the Andrew Lloyd Webber DVD. I know he's one of your favourites.

As you know, so far, being confined to our homes has been challenging, especially for Kenny. The days are long, and the weeks seem like months. Autism is definitely not a friend of this virus! As you know with Kenny's condition, he desperately needs to know what is happening, how long for and why. Just to cope basically. For someone who relies so heavily on timings and finds change so hard to cope with, he would have made you proud of how well he's coping. I've explained what I can. As his mother, I must respect he is 13 years old now, a teenager, so I have been as honest as I can. I told him there is a virus going around which can kill people, and that it is easily spread so we must keep Kenny and everyone he loves safe.

Everything Kenny used to enjoy has been taken away, and so abruptly. Absolutely, no time to prepare which is normally so vital. One day he woke up and his world changed. No school, which of course he loves. And no respite, which is vital for Kenny to develop his social skills. There's not even Carl to take him running, which as you know is his therapy. The poor boy has lost everything outside of home.

I have no idea how much Kenny understands, home schooling is difficult. He sees me as his mum, not his teacher. His brothers and sisters are not normally classed as his classmates. There is no visual schedule for each day in his blue book, no separate rooms or corridors for Kenny to walk through and to. Instead, he has our lounge with a few educational posters and a teacher who doesn't know what on earth she's doing. So, to help schooling, I have now changed his home. His sanctuary. His happy place. You might say, 'well don't do it, just cope the best you can until the storm rides out.'

But I have Kenny's brothers and sisters to think of too. I have to try and make it work for their sake.

The last few weeks Kenny has been fine, tense but overall okay. This week, however, things have changed. Kenny obviously reached his limit. He has been lashing out, slapping his brothers and sisters on the head, screaming and crying for no reason, hitting out uncontrollably and yet sitting on me every time I am sat down, or leaning on me. He wants to be holding on to me constantly. It gives me such a mix of emotions because although I feel like I am suffocating, I am filled with maternal longing to comfort him as I know he does this out of fear and desperation.

When the government announced the school closures, we felt such hope because the Prime Minister stated 'vulnerable' children could still go to school. Alas, this has turned out to be simply a mirage. The school is open for some children, but it is not the school Kenny would know. Lots of classrooms are cornered off, only two children in the whole school are there, neither of which Kenny would normally see, so it would just be incredibly confusing and no comfort whatsoever.

Food has also been challenging. With such a limited diet, the main thing Kenny enjoys is macaroni cheese. Yet it seems the entire country has decided dried pasta is something they cannot live without and the shops are bare. We spoke to every shop we could find to see if they could order it in, but they said it was virtually impossible. Nowhere has stock. So, instead, we have had to resort to cans. It doesn't sound that bad, but of course, we are only allowed three at a time, so we are spending a fortune on shopping to provide Kenny with his needs. If he doesn't have his usual food at the usual times, he will quite literally starve himself instead.

The small amount of speech Kenny had has deteriorated, and he's taken to doing things he hasn't done in years. I guess it's the same as watching films you loved as a child that brings you comfort. He's just coping as best he can.

We have been taking our one walk a day, but of course, social distancing and separating yourself by two metres is also not a friend to Autism. Spatial awareness is non-existent. We have to be careful where we take Kenny, and for such a physical boy who has a run whenever he feels stressed, to be honest, it is not even the tip of the iceberg.

There is a reason I had to get in touch Mum, you see we had news the government have changed the rules! I know you have been so worried I might not be coping too well and so I wanted to write so you could read it again and again. Things are getting better.

Thanks to our Prime Minister being so mindful on mental health, he has made allowance for people who are autistic and their carer to drive to open spaces. We couldn't believe it! We can go three times a day. It is going to make such a huge difference to us and Kenny. At last, he can have some therapy again in places he recognises. Places he feels safe. I know we can't take the rest of the kids with us, but they will feel the benefit as there will be so much less aggression in our house and they can have time with me again.

Yesterday, I took Kenny to the beach and it was incredible. We were both so excited I can tell you! Kenny just ran in the sand, relishing every ounce of freedom while I gave him space and walked along the water's edge, smelling the sea and taking in its loveliness. I had that feeling; you know when you are on holiday where you just take in the beauty and feel so lucky to have that moment. Messages were etched out in the sand, so when you walked along you felt hope and that we were in this crisis together as a nation. We were both so happy when we got back, it felt so good. I know you miss the beach Mum, but when the time comes and this lockdown is over, you will not believe how thankful for the world you become. It is such an amazing feeling.

I know I have worried you a little, but I do believe I have given you hope. Your daughter and grandchildren are okay. We will talk on the phone and skype soon. Please give my love to dad. We will go for that afternoon tea when this is all over, I promise, and I am going to hug you for such a long time!

Keep smiling mum, I love you

All my love

Cassie xxxxxx

PS. I have included some pictures of rainbows the children painted to put in your windows. They all send their love and miss you every day xxxxx

Empty Classroom

The doors are closed, to all but a few

The debate began quickly, as parents began to queue.

'Take my child! They must go to school!'

When I state 'only key workers', they become nasty and cruel.

The rooms are spiritless, asleep, joyless and still,

Those desired spaces no child wants to fill.

We do what we can to pass the day

Mostly just wishing the time away.

I sit in my classroom amongst the tables and chairs

Remembering the noise, the ideas
we shared.

So much joy the pupils bring me, as I
watch their minds grow

Learning, excitement to show me
what they know.

But now it is silent, only the keyboard
I tap

The only contact now is cyber, until it
is safe to come back.

Keyworkers are the most at risk, the
ones most in danger.

Their children are potential carriers,
as soon as they enter.

I'm scared.

Please let me stay home, I want to
be like you.

What everyone forgets is

I'm a parent too.

Celebrity

Every party is cancelled, every launch postponed because of a bat flu thing or something.
People are not interested in my posts on social media about home schooling, they just point out I haven't got any kids and that I don't know anything. My make-up line Aspire S *has been put on hold, along with my new fashion line,* Inspire S. *My calendar and social life are completely stripped bare.*

Musicians all over the world are just singing on camera phones, what am I meant to do? What am I famous for? What can I do apart from standing there, get made up and look pretty with an amazing body? I could write a book or call Jasmine to write it for me I suppose. A new novel would bring in some money, but no one goes to the shops anymore. There are no shops open.

My PA Rosie must self-isolate because her kid has a cough. She left me a whole load of hashtags to post next to my photos on Instagram. I've already uploaded pictures of myself reading my book #StayingInDoingMyBit, faking sleeping selfies in my bed #SaveOurNHS, pretending to weed the garden #LivingMyBestLife, even watching television #TogetherMyselfAndI (I made up that one, I was hoping it would start trending but no luck) and I even put some old childhood photos up there #MakingMemories. I can't think of anything else.

I don't speak to my mother, she's self-isolating with her new boyfriend, Scott, having a whale of a time. She gets more sex than me and yet she is older and fatter than I am! How is that even fair? I want a boyfriend but not a needy one, someone who appreciates what he has.

I want Rosie. I call her number.

'Hello? No! Don't touch your face! Sorry! Hold on a minute…'

I haven't even said hello yet, I hope she doesn't speak to any of my promoters like this. I look at my nails wondering if getting them done counts as an essential car trip. She's gone. I can hear 'We need to wash your hands' *in the background.*

'Hello. Who is it?'

She's back.

'Hi Rosie, it's Susanna. Susanna Poe.'

'Oh hi. Do you need something, cos I can't really…'?

'No, I'm calling for a chat.'

'A what? A chat?' *She is making this awkward.*

'Yes, I'm a bit bored.'

'You called me because you are bored?'

'Umm…yes.'

Silence.

'Susanna, I'm sorry, but I'm kind of in the middle of stuff.'

'With your kid or something?'

'Yes, Jacob. Remember he has a cough and a bit of a temperature?'

'Yeah, I remember.'

'Okay, well, I got to go.'

'Okay.'

'Can you call your mum? Or work on some stuff to promote your brands when this is all over?' *She says the kid's name again.* 'Or,' *Rosie begins a bit more brightly.* 'Have a go at online shopping if you can get a slot.'

'Online shopping? Right. Okay, I can do that. Do the Sushi people deliver?'

'I don't think they're open.'

I hear MUMMY! In the background with some coughing. The kid should really learn not to interrupt his mother when she is on the phone.

'Sorry I got to go!' *Rosie says all flustered again*. 'Good luck! See you soon!'

'Yeah, see you…' *She hung up. I didn't even say goodbye yet. I cannot believe I pay her to act like this.*

Right. Online shopping. How hard can it be?

I don't really need clothes. I try the supermarkets but can't get a slot. They are only open for vulnerable people whoever they are. Does the fact I'm alone, make me vulnerable?

I google it. `Virus. Vulnerable.`

No apparently. I must be ancient or have a load of conditions.

I google myself, but there's just a Wikipedia page and a Facebook profile of a woman in Denver. I search in images. Lots of photos of my promo shoots, magazine shoots, Instagram photos and pictures of me at parties and shopping. A couple of swimsuit shots where I look really fit. I save those to post later.

Apart from that one! What have they done!?! My face on a sheep! What on earth? Sickos.

I don't bother looking at the news, it's all rubbish. So, I decide to check out my website. It all looks quite old and has a big banner across the top of it about our position on the global plague consuming my entire world. I wasn't even aware I had a position.

I go on twitter for the tenth time that morning, then Instagram and Facebook. I put my Calvin Klein Sunglasses on and take a photo of me wearing them next to my kettle.

```
Doing the British. Carry on,
stiff upper lip and drink tea.
Don't forget the biscuits
😉
```

Taking my packet of biscuits from the cupboard, I take a quick selfie with them and the kettle. The pack is four years old and out of date, but they still look good on camera. I put the biscuits back in the cupboard on the 'show shelf' next to a pack of green tea and a box of Instant Brownie Mix when I want to give the impression I bake. That one comes out with a sealed bag of flour just to make the pictures more real. Questions like 'How do you keep in such good shape?' always pop up in interviews thanks to my little collection. Apparently, it makes me more relatable.

I post it on twitter and remind myself to check out my likes and comments over the next hour.

I wait a while and then check the post. It says it was only posted two minutes ago. I look anyway, one like. I wonder if in the course of a couple of weeks if I have become less famous. What are people doing with themselves? They should all be online; my audience figures should be through the roof. What else is there to do? I post the pic on Instagram as well hoping it will bring in more attention. I check out other people's profiles for ideas and really wish I had a baby or a dog. Those people have it so easy. I wander around my house looking for objects to take photos of.

I take a photo of my bed and then remember I posted that last week.

I google Netflix. Everyone talks about it all the time, but I don't know what the hell it is. Film and TV. Not bothered about that, no patience for it.

I call my mum. She answers the phone breathless. I quickly hang up. She's obviously having sex with that boyfriend of hers. What else could it be?

A Nurse's Duty

I grab my uniform, fresh from the machine

Trying not to think about how it will never be clean.

It stinks of loss, anger, loneliness and death.

Unforgettable patients. Every final diseased breath.

I tell myself, *Keep going, you're needed on the front line.*

Wear your mask and gown. Hopefully, you'll be fine.

I hug my children tightly, hoping it's love I project

And not the consuming fear that it is them I will infect.

This hospital is like a war zone, experts choose who lives and dies.

As the casualties of the virus rest, we
feel their terror deep inside.

We tell them to ring their families,
they may see them no more,

As reality hits them, the question of
their fate is impossible to ignore.

We clean and scrub the beds as
soon as they are clear,

We try not to count how many
bodies have been here.

The wards are silent, we try and keep
upbeat,

When my shift is over, I step out to a
deserted street.

Inside my place of work, people are
in the aisles, all around

But here outside, everything is still.
Not a soul to be found.

I find a supermarket, exhausted,
hungry, no energy to spare.

Everywhere I look the stripped
shelves are bare.

I locate an over ripe banana and
begin the drive home.

I realise I've not called my husband,
so I pull over and pick up my phone.

I tell him to remind our daughters not
to hug me or come close when I
arrive.

It breaks my heart, but I need to
shower. It's essential. Giving us a
chance to survive.

A new day awaits, a never-ending
cycle of horror, panic and danger.

I will do my duty, gambling myself,
for another. A stranger.

This is a global emergency with its
future unknown,

Help us, protect us, respect our
sacrifice.

Please.Just stay home.

STAY HOME. PROTECT THE NHS. SAVE LIVES.

A Round of Appreciation

Tom Clarke turned off the kettle and stroked his bushy beard. Another early start. He drank his cup of tea fast while his dog Han snored in his bed. Tom's bones ached and he felt he aged years in just a few weeks. Lots of postmen were off or on leave, and consequently, He had been ordered to cover a few random places on top of his usual round. There was talk of the postal service helping with shopping or delivering medicines, but that plan was scrapped when Royal Mail became busier than ever. It seemed lots of the UK population were ordering online through boredom and doing lots of shopping for home school supplies or just stuff to keep the kids busy and out of the parent's hair. He was at his usual village today, Figgy Hobbin. It was his regular route but lately, it had not felt the same.

Once a busy village full of life, the streets had become deserted. Few cars ran through the road, villagers who used to stop and chat now hid in all their homes. Tom felt lonely, shattered, and fed up.

Contamination had invaded his life. Tom always enjoyed being a postman, but he was scared now. The virus was new, the world was still learning. What's to say it couldn't be transferred through letterboxes? How long did germs stay on metal? He didn't know and was too exhausted to find out. Royal Mail had offered gloves and masks as an option to help protect their staff on routes, but Tom found wearing them too distracting and made him more uncomfortable. He carried around hand sanitiser instead which he applied after every little group of houses.

He drove to the depot and signed in before collecting the post from the allocated slot for the postcodes he needed to deliver to Figgy Hobbin and filling up his van. He walked through the village, and up the hill, his feet felt like lead. Every house was an effort. He kept his head down, he just wanted to go home. Every time Tom had a parcel, he would knock on the door loudly and then sign on the resident's behalf. One good thing about the virus was a lot more people were in, so Tom had very few parcels to take back to the depot at the end of the day. A couple of people spoke to Tom, but he kept the conversation short and was on his way quickly.

The villagers of Figgy Hobbin liked Tom, and, as they were confined to their homes, quite a few kept gazing out the window. Lizzie Rush was one of those who enjoyed people watching and would often view the world from her armchair. She saw families enjoying their one hour of exercise and some days she would see Tom. As he had not done the route for a few days, Lizzie was shocked when she saw him walk by that morning and just stared at him through the window. Tom kept his head down so thankfully did not see the sadness coming from the villager's face.

The image of Tom played in the back of Lizzie's mind and a couple of hours later when she was on Facebook, Lizzie had an idea and headed to the village Community page.

She wrote:
Did anyone else notice Postman Tom on his rounds today? He looked worn out, not like himself at all. I think the pressure's getting to him. Broke my heart ☹

Lizzie made herself a coffee, settled in her armchair and opened Facebook. She saw 7 people had already commented on her post. And 13 had either liked it or put a sad face.

Nicola Williams I saw him too. Poor Tom!

Zoe Twist ☹

Michael Swann I feel for him. He does such a good job,

always careful with my parcels, always happy to chat.

Kerry Cook Oh no! I didn't see him! We all love Postman Tom!

Stefan Harris Maybe we could all cheer him up somehow. As a village, we can all do something nice for him. When is he next on, does anyone know?

Gavin Pritchard Spoke to Tom briefly, he's here on Thursday.

By the time Lizzie had read through the replies, lots of people had reacted to Stefan's post and a few people said they were 'in'.

Lizzie typed:

Great Idea **Stefan Harris** let's all try and do something to cheer Tom up on Thursday. Get thinking people!

On Thursday, Tom made his cup of tea as usual and drank it whilst Han slept soundly in his bed. Tom had to take him out as soon as he got home from work which sometimes felt like a really hard thing to have to do. But he loved his dog dearly and wanted to take care of him during this dangerous time. Han had become Tom's lifeline. Normally he would be with his mum and dad every Sunday for a roast and catch up with them and his little sister, but due to the lockdown he hadn't been able to see them.

Being single in his own home did have the advantage food-wise. It didn't matter what he ate as long as he did, and Tom was easily pleased. By the time Tom got home, he didn't do a lot due to pure tiredness and fatigue. As soon as he left the front door, Tom wanted to be home again.

Wearily Tom drove to the depot, loaded up his van and drove to Figgy Hobbin.

He entered the village and parked his van in the usual spot on his round. The first houses he went to were elderly residents and the day felt much the same. Closed doors, quiet surroundings but then he came to the Harris family's house. There was a bottle of beer waiting for him with a post-it note attached.

For Tom x
Thank you for everything you do. Have a drink on us!
The Harris family xxx

Tom smiled as he read the note and heard tapping on the window. Staring back at him was the four Harris children smiling and waving.

'HI TOM!' they shouted. Tom laughed and waved back.

Feeling a little lighter, Tom carried on with his round.

The next two buildings were closed and silent, but then Tom came to the next house. There were painted rainbows all over the window glass and in the middle was a painting of a postman. Tom smiled and felt warmed by the sentiment.

On the next home, a game of noughts and crosses were sellotaped to the door.

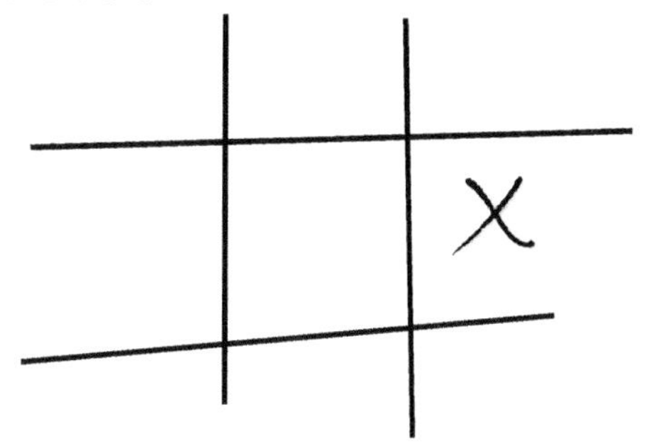

Game on Tom!

In fact, that was the first of eleven games of noughts and crosses Tom started playing that day.

When Tom came to the Pritchard house, a whole display was left out for him. There was a jam jar painted with the words *Thank you* across the face. Flowers were inside and painted stones surrounded it, with messages like '*We love our postie*' and '*Thank you Tom*'.

Zoe Twist lived on her own. When Tom came to her door, she was leaning out of her upstairs window and started clapping. Then the next house opened their upstairs window and did the same. On the opposite side of the street, windows started opening there, and Tom completed Wisteria Hill to a lengthy round of applause. At first, he was slightly taken aback and maybe a bit embarrassed, but he also felt tears as the appreciation and gratitude echoed all around him. He had never felt so overcome and valued as he did when he saw all the villagers on the street applauding and cheering his name.

The Williams household left Tom a card and a cake where the top was decorated to appear as a letter. Tom smiled and put the card into the pocket of his shorts. Tom took the cake back to his van and placed it carefully on to the passenger seat.

The Cook family had used several pieces of white A4 paper to spell out 'WE LOVE YOU

TOM!' in giant letters across their lounge window. And around the corner Michael Swann had left him a bottle of whiskey in a blue gift bag. Tom looked at the tag. '*Cheers Tom!*'

One of the final houses to visit was Lizzie Edwards. Lizzie had left a letter addressed to Tom and sellotaped it on the door. It also had 'read later' written under his name. Tom put it in his back pocket.

As he drove away from the village and back to the depot to return the van, Tom tried to let everything that had happened that day sink in. He found it hard to process it all, he never imagined he would ever have a day like today.

When Tom came through his front door, he put the bottle of beer in the fridge and the cake and whiskey on his worktop. He walked Han along the country lanes near where he lived and then came home and had some of the letter cake and a cup of tea. Afterwards, he went to the bathroom and had a long hot bath, thinking about the applause he had received, reliving the moment of Wisteria Hill. After his bath, Tom shaved off his beard and got dressed in fresh clean clothes.

He got the cold beer he was given from the fridge and opened the card from the Williams house. It was a simple message thanking him and that they hoped he enjoyed the cake. Tom put the card to the side of him, ready to display on his mantlepiece later.

He then opened the letter from Lizzie.

Dearest Tom,
Every time we see you, you brighten our day.
The world is crazy right now and it seems everyone is relying on the selected few to keep everyone going and see us through these dark times. It's a lot to put on others and when we saw the pressure

might be getting to you, as a village we decided to show you how much we appreciate the work you do and that you show up every day to make us smile.

My birthday was yesterday and right now myself and my boyfriend are apart. He lives upcountry, and without you doing your job I would not have received any cards or have the beautiful birthday card he sent down to me.

You are making a difference in people's lives. You are so valuable to so many. You are our hero, Postman Tom!

Thank you and we love you!

Lots of love,

Lizzie, Dylan (my fiancé) and all our fellow residents of Figgy Hobbin xxx

Tom sat quietly in his chair and thought. A hero. He had no idea the village community held him in such high regard.

Throughout the isolation, Tom carried on playing noughts and crosses with the eleven households that started games with him. He lost quite a few but pulled back some as well. Eventually, the quarantine lifted and the pressure on the postal workers eased. Years later, when Tom had a family of his own, he would tell his children about his perfect day as a postman. The sun shone that day but more importantly, a community came together and reminded him of how seemingly simple tasks can make such a difference to so many lives.

Nothing is greater than the power of gratitude, and letting others know their true value, especially when they are serving on the front line. Going to work for a job you do to pay the rent is transformed into a dangerous duty filled with risk, but you are now courageous, admired and brave. In short, you have become essential. Vital. But most importantly you are a part of a group of people working

together to save society. You
become your country's salvation.

Homework Report

Hollywell Class Homework

Teacher Mrs McDowell

Home report by Clara Martin
age 7 and 5 months.

My name is Clara and I have been home for, I think, 3 years 2 months and 1 day. I am lucky because I am still in Mrs McDowell's class and she is a good teacher. My homework is to write about being at home with Mummy and my brother, Charlie. We all have to stay home because people are very sick, and we might get sick too. I wash my hands a lot because

Mummy says it will make our hands too slippery for germs. We count to 20 every time we wash our hands as Mummy says that will kill the virus. Sometimes we sing happy birthday instead even though it is nobody's birthday, but it is a nice song, so I do not mind.

Mummy says we have to help Mr Netherton next door because he could be very poorly and might die like the cat from behind the fence. This is because he is old. So, we take him cake and Mummy brings him his shopping. I do not have to get dressed until almost lunchtime now every day which I like.

Mummy does read with me and yesterday we made a rocket.

We dressed up Stanley my teddy as an alien and my barbie doll, who has no clothes, a spacesuit out of toilet paper. We then had to take off all the toilet paper and wrap it around the toilet roll again. I wanted to paint it pink as it is barbie's favourite colour, but Mummy said no. Tomorrow we are painting a planet. We put glue and paper (not toilet paper) on a green balloon but it is very sticky and needs to dry. I am going to make a rainbow planet with a unicorn.

On my planet, everyone will have their own pet unicorn and eat spaghetti. And there will be no sick people on my planet or dead cats. And Mr Netherton can live there. And Granny Helen and Grandpa Joseph and Nanny

Laura and Grandad Steven too, so we can all be together and never have to be apart again.

Every day I have PE with Charlie. Mummy puts on YouTube and a man comes on called Joe. He does spiderman moves and kangaroo jumping which I like. Sometimes Mummy joins in but when she does daddy laughs at her and points which is not kind.

I play on my tablet and my friends and me play games together. Sometimes not all my friends are online, but we have fun anyway. I am the best at Dance Off and the Obbys. In the game, I have a pet unicorn called Rebekah. My friend Florrie wishes she had one too, but she has not got enough credits yet. She is not as good as me.

One day when Mummy and me and Charlie were on a walk, we passed my friend Scarlet's house and I saw her in the window. We waved to each other which was cool. I miss my friends, especially Scarlet, she is my best friend. And Mrs McDowell and Miss Rodgers who is also in my class. I miss school too but not much. I like being at home with Mummy. Daddy is home every day which is nice because we all eat lunch together. Daddy works upstairs but comes down to make coffee and eat toast.

Mummy says it is a scary time, but we need to be brave. Nurses and doctors are helping us. I am not scared because I have Stanley and I can count to 20 and sing happy birthday. Sometimes Mummy is sad. I tell her not to worry because we are okay. Everything will be fine as long as we follow the rules.

Rule 1 Stay inside

Rule 2 wash our hands

They are easy rules so it will be easy to stay safe. And then we can all be together again. And everybody will be happy.

Emmeline

I walked beside the large window; the name *Emmeline* etched in its face as it looked outwards onto the street. I took out my key and opened the door awakening my aborted journey. It feels so long since I was last here. A vast shadow stretched over every chair whilst encompassing everything from the laminated dark wooden floorboards to the rustic tabletops. The last days specials are still etched on the blackboard, its display now consisted of only faded chalk barely legible to see. Curves of letters have vanished into darkness, a cruel reminder of happier days I took for granted.

A layer of dust framed my pictures. Once they depicted famous cafes around the world, they now created an ambience of a world lost from another age. Another time that was wished for in prayers and reminisced within families torn apart by fear.

That last day was quiet. Distress and anxiety had already reached the town, and few dared to risk exposure for a slice of cake and Italian coffee. When your business is based on social gatherings, it is a cruel irony that what should bring joy, comfort and relaxation could create woe, agitation and distress. The business was hard work as I could only afford skeleton staff and I did all the baking myself. I was good at my routine and always had a full range of cakes to tempt passers-by. I was famous for my meringue pie, a different flavour every week from raspberry to rhubarb, to chocolate to lime.

When the news came from the government that all cafes had to close, I tried providing a takeaway service, just to keep the business alive. I spent a fortune on boxes online but hardly anyone came in, so I had to stop. At first, the lie-ins after the lockdown were quite nice, but I missed my routine. I missed my baking. I started to bake again and dropped cakes to elderly neighbours that could be frozen. But elderly people do not eat much, so it wasn't long before they asked me to give them no more.

I spent my days doing very little but, then I saw it. It was a news story about how, during isolation, the famous French baking chef Rene Cruz was giving free online tutorials on YouTube, and they were available with English subtitles. I was quite talented with cake but never really mastered bread. I came up with a plan to help save my business among the locals and stop myself feeling so isolated. I was going to deliver and mail order food I made. The idea was to use 24-hour services through delivery companies for the cakes which I could do countrywide for relatives and friends of customers and deliver in my car to the locals. There was not a lot of cakes I could do that would stop my range looking similar so I thought I would master bread making as well. All I had was time, which was exactly what I needed. Every day I followed Chef Rene Cruz and his video instruction until I had learnt enough to offer a solid range of bread as well as cake. Luckily for me, my brother worked at a bakery and could get me some flour and yeast on a regular basis.

As soon as I advertised my new venture for *Emmeline*, the response was electric. The orders came flooding in, and I am ferociously busy as a result. I have also had the idea of using the long-life food stock I have in the cafe as an add-on extra or as an ingredient which is why I came here. My plan was to completely empty my stock room and load it into my car. I wasn't prepared for the sadness and broken heartedness that has consumed me.

I have no idea when I will be able to return and value every hectic frenzied moment of my café, I am just relieved I have found a plan to survive. I expect the restaurants will be one of the last places allowed to re-open, so it may be a while before the shadow will be lifted. Until that long-awaited day, I will do everything I can to stay in touch with my customers.

And I hope they will look for me and my *Emmeline* when all this is over.

A Prayer from Mother Earth

Dear God,

I feel sick.

Please stop the trains, make the rails cold.

Silence the cars, turn off the engines.

Give fathers and mothers quality time with their babes.

Flood children with their parents love and protection.

I beg you, restrict consumption, lower the greed.

Show people the paradise in their gardens, the freshness around their homes, simple shades of green, the murmur of a bumblebee, the flicker of a butterfly.

I wish to ease the population. My world is becoming full.

Please lord, encourage the strong to aid the weak.

Purify my rivers, make them clear
and clean again.

Land all the planes.

Help people take care of their
health and their bodies.

Renew friendships, kinships, and
appreciation for others

Make humans remember how it feels
to hold someone, to miss someone,
to appreciate one another

Help people choose to support their
local farmers, businesses and honour
their neighbours

Restart my world

Revive my nirvana, my Eden.

And God

Please, I beg,

grant me time to heal.

Amen

Route 66

I go to the bus depot at about 6:30 am. The sun is already rising, and I realise my sunglasses are still at home. I curse at myself and head toward the office.

'Hey Buddy.' my supervisor Tim greets me as I enter to sign in.

'Hi, Tim.' I smile. 'Still here then?'

'Yep, hard to get rid of me! Have a good day today mate, alright?'

'Thanks, Tim, you too.'

Grabbing my duty board, I move towards the door so I can check the maintenance of my bus. Suzie, a fellow driver, walks in so I take a few steps back and wait to give her plenty of room.

'Morning Bud.'

'Morning Suz, have a good day.'

As she moves inside, I walk out and find my bus, number 66. I check the tyres and lights; they are all good, exactly what I expect. I've only had to alert the engineers once before. Normally they keep the buses in good shape.

I check my bag for my pack lunch and a bottle of hand sanitiser. We've all been given these screens to help protect us which fit inside of the cab, my little area. They are so flimsy though, and annoying. A lot of the guys don't think it does much to protect us. If they had solid ones maybe more of us drivers would be more enthusiastic about using them.

My round is the least wanted out of all the ones the company does. I pick up from around the city and take passengers to the hospital and back. The way I see it, I am doing a service, helping the hospital staff get to work and save lives. I've never had anyone cough on my route, so I don't feel scared or anything, you just get on with your job. Carry on like you always did. A lot of the guys feel like that. A couple are a bit nervous, but we just take it on the chin.

I turn the key as the engine jolts into life. As the welcome humming of the bus vibrates my seat, I revolve the large wheel and pull away. My job is boring now. There's no danger of being late, the roads have never been so empty since Cornwall was put on essential travel only. I used to have about forty or fifty passengers in each shift, now I have anything from only three to twelve a day. The car parks have all been made free for the NHS workers, so they tend to use them instead, most probably consider it safer than being on public transport.

At the train station I pull over into the layby for the bus stop. My friend is waiting for me, we see each other every day. He comes on my bus after a long train journey from his home. There's only one big hospital in Cornwall, so the staff come from all over. He then goes to work and then catches the bus to the station and takes the long train journey back again. He does that every day. He's not young either. Quite old really, definitely around the retirement age.

'Morning Leslie' I greet him as he climbs on.

'Hiya Buddy. The sun's shining well today, lovely views on the ride in.' Leslie replies as he scans his bus pass, he lets out a sneeze and takes the seat across from me so we can chat. Leslie's the only passenger so far. It's not unusual at this time of the morning.

'Yep, you can't beat Cornwall when it's like this. Gorgeous place to live.'

'Makes you feel blessed to be here.' Leslie holds on tightly to the top of a pillowcase. Due to hospital regulations, he carries his scrubs inside it.

'Without a doubt. Busy day today?'

'Won't know until I get in there.' Leslie works in the X-Ray department. Most infected patients get x-rayed because of what it does to your lungs.

'There was a guy who came in last week, did I tell you?' Leslie adds.

'Not sure.'

'Well, I knew him from school!' Leslie laughs. 'Not seen him in absolute decades. Couldn't believe it.'

'Blimey, it is a small world!' I laugh. 'Do you know how he's doing?'

Leslie turns to the window beside him, furthest away from me. 'Yeah, Mary from his ward told me. He didn't make it.'

'Ah, I'm sorry mate.'

'It happens. We had a good chat while he was there. No one could be with him you see, because of the virus and that.' Leslie fiddled around in his pocket and pulled out a hanky. He sneezed again.

'I know it's against regulations, but I gave him a hug I did.' His voice cracks a little as he speaks. I say nothing and let him go on when he's ready. 'Just felt so sorry for him, Bud, we were pretty good mates a few years ago.'

'They do say, we will all know one person affected, don't they? Maybe that's your one.' I try and reassure him.

'I've had a few mates, one of the downfalls of being an old man.'

'You're not that old, Leslie.'

'I'm seventy next month.' He gets out his hospital ID and holds it in his hand.

'How come you are still working?'

'What else am I going to do?'

'Knit?' I suggest as we both laugh.

Leslie sneezes again into his hanky.

'You got a cold?' I ask.

'Little bit. Ah, I'll be alright.'

We get to the hospital and he climbs off.

'Take care of yourself, Leslie.'

'You too, Buddy. Thanks, mate.' He picks up the pillowcase and flings it over his shoulder.

We wave goodbye as he heads through the doors into the building.

There are no other passengers on my route and I eat my packed lunch in the depot.

I drive around the city and pick Leslie up with another passenger around teatime. After taking them back to the station, I head back to the depot for home. As we had another passenger, Leslie automatically sits halfway down the bus and stares out of the window.

The next day there is no Leslie. In all the times I have done the 66 route he has never missed a day. The same went for the next shift and the one after. I didn't see him for a few weeks. Then I develop a cough and have to self-isolate. When I run a temperature and find it hard to breathe, I am admitted to the hospital. I ask about Leslie and the doctors and nurses promise they will find out for me. I am still waiting to hear just before they induce me into a coma.

PM Cleaner

The unimaginable had happened. A highly contagious virus was let loose all over the world and thanks to the speaker at the House of Commons, the whole Houses of Parliament had caught it and was now isolating. The day was not a lucky one for Barbara Cavill, every other member of the Borough Cleaning Company team for the Houses of Parliament was off and it was down to her to do all the work. It took her all day now, although no one was in the building which made it easier, and she didn't even bother wearing her uniform. No one was there to see it.

The day was not going to get better. Unknown to Barbara, Rory Fisher was filling in for the head of PR for 10 Downing Street, Gaynor Mayfield, as she was also self-isolating.

Rory's first job was to go to the Houses of Parliament and find an MP to become temporary Prime Minister whilst the whole cabinet was off sick.

It was a top priority getting someone to fill in as leader of the country as the whole of the UK was panicking and looking for someone to lead. As Rory entered the building, the only person he could find was Barbara.

Rory approached her and said quickly 'Can you work at Number 10?'

'Which floor is that? I do it all mate!'

'I mean Number 10 Downing Street.'

Barbara always thought Number 10 Downing Street looked quite small from the footage on the telly. 'Will I get double time?'

Rory didn't know what that meant but due to the urgency of his task, he thought it wouldn't be a problem.

'Sure. Just come now.'

'If you want me to come now, I need triple time.'

'I'm sure that will be fine just come now.'

'Okay. Let me get my stuff.'

That was easier than I thought! Rory mused.

Barbara disappeared and Rory picked up his phone and dialled Gareth, his boss. 'I found someone! They can start right away.'

'Brilliant Rory! Fantastic work. Come back to number 10 and I'll call the press, tell them to get here sharpish as our new Prime Minister is on the way. What's their name?'

'Oh! I don't know!' Rory looked to the side. 'Oh! Wait a minute, they're coming back.'

Barbara was walking towards Rory with a backpack.

'I'm so sorry. What's your name?'

'Barbara Cavill. I'm with the Borough. The BCC.'

'Oh okay. Her name is Barbara Cavill, she's part of the Borough.'

'BCC.' Barbara interrupted.

'BCC.' Repeated Rory into the phone.

'Yes, don't worry, the BBC will be on their way. Get here quick as you can Rory. Good work.'

'Thank you.' Rory turned off his phone and turned to Barbara. 'Ready?'

'Yes. My trolley is just over here.'

'Trolley?'

Barbara walked over to a cleaning trolley. 'Yes, my stuff is just here.'

Rory stared at the cleaning trolley, polish, duster and rubber gloves. And then at Barbara. His eyes widened as he made the connection and he struggled to talk.

Barbara touched him on the arm. 'Are you okay? You're really pale.'

Rory struggled to find the words. 'Are you...'

'Did you want to sit down?'

'Are you a cleaner?'

'Yes, of course, you want me to clean number 10. Triple time don't forget.'

'I thought you were an MP.'

Barbara laughed. 'A what? MP? No, they're all off with the Koala-virus. All my team are off too. There's only me left now.'

'Jesus Christ! You don't even know what it's called! Oh my God!' Rory took out his phone and called Gareth.

He answered on the first ring. 'Rory! Are you on your way? Everybody's coming.'

'No, I've not left yet...'

'What!?! Get over here right away! That's an order!' Gareth hung up.

Rory put away his phone. 'Oh my God.'

Barbara came a bit closer to him. 'It's okay. It can't be that bad. Is there anything I can do?'

'Yeah, become an MP,' answered Rory spitefully.

'Might take some time,' smiled Barbara.

'That's the one thing I haven't got. They need me back at number 10.'

'Well, I said I'm ready. I have my gear. Hopefully, no one will find out, I'm doing that job as well as this one. I don't want to get into trouble. We can pretend, can't we? No one will know.'

'Pretend.'

'Yeah, so I keep my job.'

'Maybe we can pretend so we can both keep our jobs.'

'I'm not following.'

'Barbara, I need you to become Prime Minister.'

'I'm sorry?'

'It's okay, no one will check, everyone's just desperate for a leader.'

'I'm no Prime Minister!'

'You could have a prime minister's salary.'

Barbara stopped.

Rory leant in. 'Do you know what a Prime minister makes?

'No.'

'Just less than 150 grand.'

'I would get paid that?'

'If you come now you will.'

Barbara's head filled with ideas. No mortgage, no debt, a holiday abroad. New kitchen and bathroom. Everything she's ever wanted but never believed could ever happen. 'What would I need to do?'

Rory led her by the arm. 'I'll tell you in the car.'

Rory and Barbara were greeted by a mass of cameras, microphones, Dictaphones, arms and bodies. As the car pulled up Gareth opened the door. Rory had given Barbara his suit jacket in the car as he briefed her. Rory was 6ft and broad-shouldered, but Barbara was quite small at just 5ft 5. Her hands disappeared inside the arms and the jacket came just above her knees.

'Are you sure I look okay? It's a bit big!'

'You're fine! Just do it up.' Rory leant over and pulled the sides together.

Before, Barbara had just jeans and a t-shirt on. With the jacket done up, it covered most of the t-shirt which featured a lovely motif /design of a porg. An adorable creature featured in the Star Wars franchise.

Gareth understandably was a bit taken aback at the MP which

looked like a child playing dress-up with Daddy's clothes.

'Barbara Cavill MP? Thank goodness you are here. Thank you for answering the call to help your country.'

'No problem.' Barbara said in the deepest most serious voice she could.

Gareth looked at her. To help ease his concern, Barbara gave him a thumbs-up, but that only seemed to make his face look worse. Gareth looked at Rory who was grinning as wide as humanly possible and even more worryingly to Gareth, he followed Barbara's example and gave him a thumbs-up as well.

Lots of voices were calling Barbara's name.

Gareth leaned into Barbara's ear and spoke quietly. 'Right, let's get started. There's no time to brief you as everyone got here incredibly fast. Just do the best you can, and we'll sort out damage control afterwards if we need to.'

Gareth took her by the arm and lead her to the famous black door of number ten. Moving her into prime position, he whispered, 'Okay, here we go,' and then stood in front of her.

'Barbara Cavill has kindly agreed to serve her country for the good of the nation.' He began. 'She will say a few words and then we'll take a very short period of questions. Please remember Barbara is very much in at the deep end here so to speak, so we would appreciate a little leniency from the press. Publicity packs will be made available to you very shortly. For now, as you may know, Barbara is from the Borough and she is very honoured to take up the post in these desperate times, and the nation thanks her. Barbara?'

Barbara stepped forward. 'Hello, everyone. Thank you for the kind welcome. The Koala-virus is a bastard.'

Gareth gave a very abrupt look to Rory who pretended not to feel his boss's eyes staring into him.

The press, however, loved the beginning and were leaning in, making sure they didn't miss a second.

'My ex-husband was a bastard.' Barbara went on. 'And do you know what I did? I sent him on his way. Sure, this virus isn't having it away with slapper Doris down the road, but it is still a bastard and so we must do the same to the bastard virus as I did with my bastard husband. We must get rid of it. The easiest way is to stay in and watch the telly. If you do go out to meet up with your mates or even with your mum and dad, then I'm sorry but you are a bastard too. Stay inside! Thank you.'

Silence.

Rory stepped forward. 'Any questions?'

The press all became an accumulation of noise.

'Maybe one at a time? Yes Anna, BBC.'

'Hi Barbara, that's quite an opening speech.'

'It needed to be said,' replied Barbara.

'And you are aware you are live across the nation?'

'Yep.'

'Okay,' smiled Anna. 'So, what measures for protective equipment are being put in place to help overrun hospitals and A&E staff?'

'You mean masks and stuff?'

'If you like.'

'I'm glad you asked that because I have a few ideas.'

Gareth glared at Rory.

Rory again pretended not to notice.

'Go on,' said Anna with a big smile.

'Okay.' Barbara began. 'We need to make masks using whatever materials we can. Knitters, Women Institutes, Pool canvas people, clothing people. The shops are shut, start manufacturing masks and aprons. If everyone who has access to materials up and down the country pulls their finger out and get sewing, we can get loads more to the right places. '

'Okay,' said Anna.

'Secondly' started Barbara.

'Oh right. Sorry. There's more.'

'I think and a lot of people agree with me that it's ridiculous that NHS staff are so poorly paid, so since all the MPs are off anyway and not working, all their wages for the time they aren't at work can be given as a bonus to NHS workers.'

'Do you include yourself in that Barbara.'

'Well, I'm the prime minister, not an MP now.' Barbara said smugly to laughter. 'And the footballers too. There are no games on. And every highly paid person who cannot work because of the virus. Their wages for the time they are off will instead go to the people who are saving us from this crisis. The ones at the frontline. The NHS.''

'Brilliant' said Anna writing it all down. 'And...'

'Sorry, just one question Anna if you don't mind,' said Gareth. 'Richard, ITV.'

'Hi Barbara, you are certainly saying what people want to hear, but are you just giving us empty promises? And, when can the public expect an end to lockdown?'

'I don't make promises I don't keep. And that next question is kind of self-explanatory, isn't it? We go out of lockdown when it is safe. People are dying for goodness sake.'

'Right. Umm...thanks.'

Gareth pointed at another. 'Stephen.'

'Hi, Barbara. What makes you think you are qualified to lead the country? What will you do differently?'

'To be honest with ya, there's no one else is there. I stepped up because my country needed me to. End of. I'm no better or worse than anyone else, but I work hard, and I know my own mind. Surely that's all we can ask for. None of us wants this, we're all just trying our best to cope and not think the worst. Times are hard, we just must pull together and do the best we can. I can't do a worse job than anyone else.

Let me put it this way, after the bastard has been tamed, our country is never going back to the way it used to be. The world has changed, and we have all changed with it. Yeah, we're all scared, but we're also all a little stronger than before. Think of the virus like a ring after a wet cup being on a nice wooden table. If you act quickly, do all the right things you can limit the damage and the table is in pretty good shape. The stain will be around for a long time and you will always know it's there but if we are lucky it will not affect anything too badly and we can use the table much as we did before. We got to keep using that polish, giving the table a nice treatment or two and then in time the ring will fade. Thank you and good night!'

Rory put on his sunglasses as the sun moved away from the cloud and blazed down on his face. Barbara put her hand up and turned to walk through the door. It was locked.

Family Extensions

Aaron

When we first heard at DK Francis Funeral Directors about the disease on the news, our first thought was fear. Everything about it was new, we had no information. And it left us terrified. I was on call for weeks, venturing into people's houses to collect the deceased after they had just passed away. Relatives were there from the scene of death, the virus still in their breath, there was a strong possibility they were carriers. I never told Karen, my wife, about them being there or how much it affected me. Being in a room with the immediate family and the body in a situation like that is a lot to take. You are stepping into a room filled with danger and death. On the outside, we treated the deceased with the same dignity and respect as anybody else, I would not compromise my standards on any level. But on the inside, I am not ashamed to say, I am afraid every time we know the cause of death is from the virus.

We are completely covered from head to toe for our own protection, so you do feel safe and looked after. You must believe that to get through it. After moving the body, we get rid of everything. When I get home, Karen is usually still in bed but not sleeping.

The other situation that is hard is when we go into care homes. They take our temperature as we come in. You feel surrounded by germs. It's not until you are in care homes that you realise how hard it must be for the staff every day. Their health, lives even, are vulnerable every second they are in there. I don't envy them at all. That's a lot harder job than mine.

Rules and guidelines change every day from the government and the company I work for. Sometimes the changes are quite drastic, we can't sit in cars with customers anymore. We used to meet with loved ones, build a relationship with the family. We would fulfil their wishes, do the person who had passed away justice. We would make them proud. We would become part of their journey. The job satisfaction came from seeing them through the worst time of their lives. Show them they were stronger than they thought. They could get through this, process their grief and longing. We were here for them. We would talk about their loved one, what made them laugh, cry, what made them who they were. We would be the pillar of strength they needed. The person they wouldn't have to think about. They were so important to us and anything we could do was never too much trouble.

We don't see the family now, we miss them. Being with them was our job satisfaction. Now we only hear a voice at the end of a telephone. The day I get to sit down face to face again, see them light up as we chat about their relative, describe the good things, funny little quirks no one else would know. Watch them as their relation comes alive in their memories as we talk. When I get to see them smile for the first time since their loss, that is the moment I am waiting for.

Karen

As soon as I heard Aaron's phone, my body would tense. I would be petrified from the moment he left our bed until he was home taking a shower. He would always be quiet when he got back. So talkative usually. As we both work in the same field, I did take some comfort as I knew he was being taken care of. Our company is very good to its employees, safety would be paramount. He obviously had it rough. Just a very intense situation, I guess. My friend Ann said her partner Jamie came home the other night and just broke down crying. Right there in the bathroom, so I know it's not been good.

My job isn't as severe as Aarons, I work in the office. One day on my way to work, I was stopped by the police. Luckily, we have documents from the government that states we are key workers, our company told us to carry those letters with us everywhere. I'm so glad I did. A lot of people forget about funeral care being key workers, no one likes to think of it I suppose. What happens to all those figures in the death tolls, what they actually mean.

When I get into work, I use anti-bacterial wipes to sanitise everything, from bannisters to computer keys. Everything a human hand has touched. I tend to deal with calls from families, the rules have all changed now.

No cars, we can't have more than a few people at services, one crematorium stopped letting people in altogether and announced it just a couple of days before the funeral. You are not allowed to sit with the deceased now, which usually brings so much comfort. Especially if it is a child that has died.

We can't dress people who have passed away which actually is a huge thing for so many families. Yet, everyone I have spoken to has been lovely and really accepting when I tell them the restrictions. They understand there is nothing I can do. I felt uncomfortable at first, sad that I had to put limits and boundaries on something that should be all about them and what they need at the service to express their loss.

We always suggest a celebration of their life later. So, you can do what they would have wanted.

Lay them to rest so they have time to grieve but have a get together later. Of course, all these conversations have been on the phone. That is the hardest part.

Clients are our family; we would do the utmost for our family. It is meeting new clients and doing everything we can to make the whole process as painless as it can be that gives us the most joy. Both myself and Aaron, and even all our colleagues feel the same way.

We get to guide you. It is not our job. It is our honour.

'Stay at Home! M.U.M!'

10:22 am

Muriel Ursula Mumford sat in her chair whilst her children's heads were buried on tablets and her husband was working in his makeshift office, formerly known as the garage. She had cleaned everywhere. Repainted the windows and doors throughout the house, the fascias, the garden gate, even the cover for the electric meter. Muriel Mumford had completed every odd job she could think of that they could not be bothered to do before. She was now grateful for something to distract her from the hellish situation inside her home.

Her children were housebound 24 hours a day. Of course, she loved them dearly, but the precious time she had to herself whilst they were at school had vanished. Along with the ability to go to the toilet on her own at any time of the day. She had taken to having a large glass of red wine most lunchtimes, the children were officially on Easter school holiday and as far as Muriel was concerned, so was she. Muriel knew the worst was coming. Home school. But best not to think about that. At least not quite yet.

Just one hour and thirty-odd minutes before lunchtime could begin.

11:30 am was too early. She could probably get away with 11:45 am though. One hour twenty-three minutes left.

The sun was out but it had a bit of a breeze. When she had got dressed this morning, it looked warm and hot, so she dressed for the summer. But of course, windows can be deceiving, and her bare legs and her arms were now covered in goose-pimples. Never mind, she would soon warm up. A glass of Merlot always tends to help in that regard.

Most parents will be working their way through Netflix right now thought Muriel, *they would be watching family films, maybe even playing a board game all together like in an advert or something.*

'Oh my god! STOP KILLING ME! YOU STUPID TABLET. I HATE YOU!' the youngest child screamed at the mechanical device.

Not idyllic advert status here. Muriel desperately wanted to watch last night's Dragon's Den, but all three children insisted on preschool kids' TV Channel CBeebies being on despite all their eyes being cemented toward the screens of their tablets. Cbeebies was fine at the bedtime hour, especially if someone dishy like Tom Hardy was reading the bedtime story, but all day, every day? It was a bit much.

Could she get away with more chocolate? She had already devoured half of the family size Galaxy bar from her stash in the kitchen cupboard. Verona, the middle child almost caught her yesterday. She had tried doing it silently with her usual military precision but somehow the kid's hearing seemed to be enhanced with all the screen time and her daughter Verona appeared faster than Usain Bolt.

'Mum?' she said, freezing her mother in seconds. 'Are you chewing?'

With her mouth full and cheeks bulging, Muriel replied as clearly as she could.

'Nftoo'

Verona pointed with her skinny arm outstretched. 'You are! What are you eating!?! Tell me right now what is inside your mouth!'

Muriel had three choices.

One.

Admit defeat and bribe her daughter with a bit of the treasured bounty. Frankly, this is the last resort. We don't know when we can get to the shops for more Galaxy chocolate.

Two.

Resort to trying to swallow the mouthful whole to prove her daughter was wrong. This could create a choking hazard of course, but with the children being home

24/7 indefinitely, choking might be a welcome relief.

Three.

Lie about what she was eating. This was by far the easiest and most promising option.

Through pure luck, Verona had walked in on her mother when she was making dinner. With a smooth gesture, Muriel felt around the worktop behind her back until she found what she'd been looking for.

Muriel chewed and swallowed. 'Okay, you caught me. I was eating this.'

Muriel showed her daughter a large spearhead of green.

'Raw broccoli. Did you want some?'

Verona stuck her tongue out in disgust. 'Urgh! No! That's disgusting! God, Mum you are so weird!'

Muriel smiled at the memory. She had told the kids when they spotted the bar of Galaxy in the cupboard, it was the emergency bar and the whole country was rationing. It wasn't a complete lie; the supermarkets have been limiting people to 3 of each item. That's rationing. Muriel had told all three children every bit of food had to go before they could touch the bar of chocolate. Experience had shown Muriel that they were gullible at this age and believed everything their parents tell them. She had stacked three of the Galaxy family size bars together and put a box of breadsticks in front of it to disguise it, but the eagle-eyed little monsters saw the edge of the wrapper and immediately knew it was chocolate.

Yet, if there is a helicopter in the sky flying about and Muriel points it out, they will not spot it no matter how loud or how close it becomes.

She had already given in to the fact she was going to be massive by the end of the lockdown. They will need a crane to get her out of the house. So, she believed she might as well go along for the ride and enjoy her temptations in gigantic proportions. No one knew who was going to get this potentially fatal disease, you don't want to be lying in the hospital wishing you ate that last row of chocolate.

'Mum! Can I have some crisps?'

Muriel answered automatically. 'Yes.'

'There's none I like! Nathaniel ate them all!' Muriel sighed at the tedious argument that took place every day. She already knew what was coming.

'I didn't eat them!' Nathaniel didn't eat them.

'George then!' Of course, it is George. It is always George.

'Food is there to be eaten.' The culprit protested. 'Mum! Can I have some crisps?'

'Yes.'

'Mum, what can I have?' Verona's voice had that irksome whiney element now.

'Fruit?'

'No!' Ironically, suggesting fruit is always fruitless. Muriel thought and then smiled to herself, wondering if she should write it as a status on

Facebook. On reflection two seconds later, she decided it sounded a bit pants and didn't bother.

'Breadsticks?' Muriel suggested.

'Cool, thanks.' The whine has vanished into a chirpier reply.

Muriel went to get up.

'Don't worry mum I can get them.'

'Thanks love.' Already Muriel knew this was a mistake.

Things crashed to the floor; the unmistakable sound of glass being smashed travelled through the lounge toward Muriel's armchair.

'Oh, for fuck's sake!' Up she got.

Maybe 11:40 am is an okay time to have wine. Surely it must be close to that now.

Muriel looked at her watch. 10:49. Shit!

World Doctors: Life on the Front Line

UNITED KINGDOM

I am terrified of losing my patients and passing the disease to my husband and children. I leave the house every day, report for duty in A&E (Accident & Emergency) and begin my long shift. I am 32 and I see patients my age, people in 30s and 40s who are health conscious, take regular exercise and yet they are in our hospital, fighting for their lives in the ICU (Intensive Care Unit). We wear our protective equipment, which is basically a mask and an apron, and between myself and my colleagues, we have to make very gruelling decisions, like which patients will have the best chance if they get to be the one to have a ventilator.

A&E is full of people with breathing difficulties. Heart attack and car crash victims are in the paediatrics department, a place which is meant to cater for children. Every member of staff is getting new training on ventilators as that is the main way we can save lives. In the UK, we have had to turn the London ExCel Centre into a makeshift hospital, soon Birmingham and Manchester will have one too. It's all so we can cope with demand with the influx of cases coming in from the big cities. We are screaming at people to stay in their homes. Those makeshift hospitals should be enough to show people how much the NHS is struggling to cope.

SPAIN

My friend and colleague, who is also a doctor at Hospital de Sant Pau, became unwell at the end of his shift. He had the classic symptoms; a sore throat, headache, dry cough, shortness of breath, everything they say to look out for on the news. It was out of concern for his family that he got tested. He told me he was even feeling a bit relieved when the test came back positive. He just hated going to work and facing another day at the hospital. That is how bad it is in there.

ITALY

People were once envious of us, getting to live in Italy. It was always regarded as a beautiful place to spend your life. For generations, my family have lived in Lucca, my home. My beautiful Nonna, the patriarch of my family has to hide away because she is too old. It is not safe for her outside. It breaks my heart.

My country is a form of perdition, an eternal suffering. I see twenty cases a day, the reasons for admission is always the same. Fever, breathing difficulties, fever and cough, respiratory failure. They all have need to be hospitalised, their tests always come back with pneumonia.

Ventilators are now like the ultimate treasure to be won. In Italy, we all are very into spending time with family and being together, but I have not seen mine since this destructive hell started. I hope one day I can be with my family without fear, that Nonna can be with her grandchildren and great grandchildren and my beautiful country can become a paradise again. How many people must die before that can happen, will I still be here to see it?

UNITED STATES OF AMERICA

Every day I am met with long lines of people on the sidewalk, a mass congregation frantic to receive our care. I am an Otolaryngologist, an Ear, Nose and Throat doctor. Normally I only deal with mild treatments, but I'm having to do multi-organ failure procedures that are really complicated. The whole situation is insane.

The bed situation is crazy. We have fifteen beds in the intensive care unit for patients with breathing difficulties, these are completely full of people with this dreadful disease. Patients are lying on the floor all over the ER and the rest of the hospital because there is nowhere for them to go.

We try to protect ourselves the best we can as there isn't enough protective gear to go around. It is always a big issue on the President's press briefings and we always hear supplies are on their way. For now we make do by bringing in goggles and face shields from home, tear up scrubs, even use hairnets if we have them. Basically, anything we can think of for added protection. We must throw away the gear we use after every patient, so if you think of the number of people we see, you can imagine how much stuff that would be. We are terrified.

I see all ages, but the majority of patients are aged anything between 30 and 70. People are dying young because of mild pre-conditions like asthma. Normally just one or two people die in a day in the hospital, now the average amount is twelve! People are dying alone in induced comas, no family, no wife or anything. The world is a scary place right now and it feels like we have put ourselves right in the most dangerous place imaginable.

GERMANY

Just under 200 seriously ill patients from other European Union countries have come to our hospital for help since the virus outbreak. We have room for more. Europe must stand together. We are here when our friends need us.

The Bundestag gives us more beds, doubling them in intensive care so we can carry on helping other countries. My colleagues are becoming infected or need to self-isolate. I want to help as my President suggests, I know this is the time we must be kind and helpful to one another, but I am also cautious of my health.

FRANCE

I answered my calling and came out of retirement to help my colleagues. Everyone was so severely overworked, I had to keep going in. I started to help at the very beginning of the outbreak, I wanted to help. The last couple of shifts I have been struggling heavily with fatigue. I do not know how I contracted the virus, but I am very ill now, and do not have much time left. There are many things I would like to do one last time, visit Provence with fields of sunflowers and lavender. There is little possibility I will see such beauty again, but my neighbour pushed some lavender she grows on her windowsill under my door.

I am not sorry I answered the call and came back. Being a doctor is my life, I had to support my friends and team. So many have been at breaking point so many times, there are so many patients coming in every day. I have no regrets.

CHINA

When the People's Republic finally confirmed what us doctors suspected, that the virus was transmitted through human contact, we already had three times our normal volume of patients. So many of my colleagues have become sick and I have lost friends. I have transferred patients to different departments, and they have died before they even got there. We see many that only come when they are too sick for us to try and save. We are really worried about a second outbreak of the virus, even if we get this wave under control, how are we going to survive another?

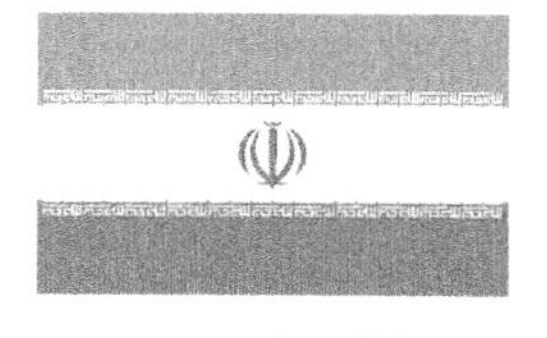

IRAN

I am very sick. I am treating patients while being connected to an IV drip, as there are not enough medical staff to help people, and there is a severe lack of basic equipment to protect us. Fifty people are being infected every hour. We all feel so helpless. I will treat my patients until my dying breath.

BRAZIL

With so many people living so densely together in Rio and so many favelas with little sanitation, our country's people are struggling. The Ministry of Health have stopped reporting the numbers of suspected cases to stop the panic, but there are many more deaths than the ones being reported.

People should know.

It feels like we have not seen the worst of this evil disease, and both myself and the staff are all worried about running out of protective equipment. We are lacking the ability to test many patients, so we send mild symptoms home. But people are scared and

refuse to leave the waiting room
which is full of the virus.

If they didn't already have the virus, the chances are they will have it when they leave.

Every day as doctors we face an impossible choice.
None of us wants to be here.

None of us ever imagined we would be dealing with anything as monstrous as this contagious beast.

If we don't turn up,
we lose our job.
What we trained for, what we based our whole lives around.

Being a doctor is part of who we are, our identity.

But if we do turn up,

if we do what we were born to do and what we all love. We could die.

One more thing...

The Contagion of 2020 spread faster than anyone living had seen before. And much of the world stopped.

As our existence became a target, vulnerable people in every country looked to their leaders for guidance. Doctors and nurses were regarded as heroes in blue, but their long-overdue recognition was at a dangerous cost. They provided the public with an unpayable debt and displayed more courage than the most valiant superhero.

Death tolls were never more sought, countries and their people united by singing on balconies to each other, sending one another messages of hope and alliance. People re-evaluated their lives as humanity was stripped bare. Affection had never been more missed, and friendships never more valued.

The devastation caused by this infection was rapid and unrelenting. Everyone was catapulted into unfamiliar territory. The most important action above all others was the safety of every nation and a vaccine became the holiest of grails every nation went on a quest to find.

It is unlikely we will ever see anything like this again. But if you are reading this you are still here, you made it. You are a survivor. We never expected such large losses, yet each fatality on the death toll died before their time. Many without family or loved ones by their side in their final moments.

You have a future now because you are strong. The world was under attack and you overcame the danger. A silent global serial killer of young, old, healthy and sick. A murderer of hundreds of thousands of people but you are still here.

You are a force to be reckoned with. A survivor. Keep fighting.

Acknowledgements

A book is never accomplished alone, so I have a few thankyous to make.

First, my friend and editor Anita Hunt. Without your brilliant insights, encouragement and excellent edits, this would be a very different book indeed. Thank you for all your help, time, and patience. How you fitted it in between writing your book, editing others, making signing videos on YouTube, and continue working with adults with additional needs, I will never know! The donation of your time and expertise to help me raise money for such a good cause is greatly appreciated.

Thank you to Stephen Murphy, Richard Swann, Steve Jones and Patricia Chapman for your valuable insights and vital roles as keyworkers during this crisis. Thank you for letting me quiz you so I at least sounded like I knew a little of what I'm talking about. I hope I didn't pound you with too many endless questions!

You are all absolute legends and I am in your debt.

Thank you to Gavin, Archie, Eliza and Hugo for all your support and for giving me time to work on this project. Especially at dinnertimes when I sat on our front lawn for hours trying to let the words flow, and for all your enthusiasm for this project. I hope you are all happy with the result.

Thank you to my beloved Mum, Don and Grampie for helping me along the way and always believing in me. I know you are watching.

Thank you to time, due to this digital age, access to information all over the globe has made research so much easier.

Thank you to all the key workers for keeping our country running, especially those on the front line. You are all superstars whose brilliance reaches beyond the realm of the galaxy.

And finally, to you, the reader. By purchasing this book, you have donated to our National Health

Service (NHS) in the UK and indulged me by stepping into my imagination and embraced my brainchildren. I hope you enjoyed reading this little book as much as I enjoyed creating it. Thank you and stay safe.

#ThankYouNHS

About the Author

Melanie Stephens is a full-time writer of fiction. She publishes a variety of short stories and poems regularly on her author Facebook page and posts on her blog Geek Girl Eats Cake.

Melanie lives in Cornwall with her husband and three children. This is her first published novella. She is thrilled it is for such a good cause.

You can follow or read more of Melanie's work on:

Facebook @melaniestephenswriter

Blog
https://geekgirleatscake.home.blog/

Printed in Great Britain
by Amazon